Disclaimer

The following is a work of fiction. All characters, events, and locations described in this book are part of the author's creative mind. Any resemblance to people, locations, or names is entirely coincidental. This book has been copyrighted and cannot be used without the author's written consent.

Dedication

This book is dedicated to my mother, the strongest woman in the world, without apology. Without her strength and prayers watching over my steps, I wouldn't be the woman I am today.

To my husband, who is my rock and support in everything I do, thank you for holding us together through every venture.

To my four daughters, whom I hope will grow up in a world more conscious of their easily broken natures as women

Table of Contents

Chapter 1 - Stitch

"Wahhhh! Wahhhh!"

"Jan, did you hear that?"

I shrugged my lady Janice, who was lying beside me on the floor. She didn't move.

"Janice," I called out to her again.

"How can she sleep that hard in this cold weather?" I thought to myself.

I listened to the noise, but everything was quiet, so I lay back down. As soon as I got back to sleep, I heard it again. The sound was so loud this time that it pierced my ears.

"WAHHHHHH! WAHHHHHH!"

"Jan, wake up! You don't hear that noise?"

"Nah, Stitch, now leave me alone and let me sleep!" she mumbled and rolled back over.

It was very cold, and I didn't want to get up, but the howling noise kept coming. I had heard a lot of strange noises when I was in the military doing tours overseas, but this noise was weird enough that I couldn't ignore it.

The bite of the bitter cold was hard to fight off. It found its way under layers of blankets and straight to my bones, even though I was fully clothed. I didn't want to move, but the noise wouldn't let me go back to sleep, so I reluctantly got up. I walked out the back door that was barely hanging onto the hinges of the old abandoned house Jan and I were squatting in.

The noise grew louder and more intense as I walked onto the porch—louder than the howling winds. My bones shivered with each step I took. Finally, I could hear the noise clearly. As I inched forward in the dark and cold, I realized it was a baby's cry.

My breath was thick in the frozen air, and I began to walk faster to locate the noise, praying it would not stop. After a few seconds, the noise disappeared, and my heart dropped.

"Shoot! Shoot! Don't go quiet now!"

Just when I thought all hope was lost, the cry came again. I looked over at the back of a building and walked towards the cry until I saw a bundle of blankets next to a trash can. I bent down and gently pulled the blanket aside and saw an infant.

"Oh, my Lord!"

I opened the blanket a little more. But just enough to see the small face of a baby with strikingly silver eyes. The baby began to shake as the cold wind hit its face. I closed the blanket quickly and gently picked it up, holding it close to my chest and running back to the house. Walking into the house, I opened the blanket again to get a better look. A note fell out that read:

"God forgive me."

The baby was no longer crying. She looked up at me with her bright and unafraid eyes. "I got you, little angel," I whispered. "I ain't gonna let nothing happen to you."

"Well, I guess I'm putting my army skills back to work," I said to myself, laying the little angel down next to Janice.

They called me Stitch in the day because I could stitch anything together to make it work. This old house was solid but lacked the warmth this baby needed. I worked all night to get it together. Janice didn't move as I worked, and the baby slept quietly.

"What were you up to all night, and why is it so warm here?" Janice asked as she woke up the following day.

"I rigged some wires together from the poles to get the electricity on and then rigged the old furnace to get the heat going," I said proudly.

"For what?" Janice asked, looking confused.

"For her," I picked up the sleeping angel from the makeshift bed made from crates and blankets. Janice stared at me and the silver-haired, silver-eyed baby for a few seconds and rolled over to sleep.

****

The first month was the hardest. We didn't have much and were unprepared to care for a baby. We considered taking her to Child

Protective Services despite the horrific things I had experienced when I was a kid in the system. I thought they could at least give her a warm home and food. But the thought of something terrible happening to her in one of those foster homes made me decide against it.

Janice and I did everything to make the abandoned house a home for our little angel. I stole all the necessities from the local stores and made sure the baby girl had milk and cereal, even when we went without food. The silver-eyed baby wasn't hard to care for because she never cried, which I thought was odd.

One night, when it got really bad, Janice and I walked to UH

Hospital in the middle of the night because we didn't have any food for her. The hospital was about a mile from our house. It was freezing, and buses had stopped running for the night. The bitter cold hit us with every step we took, but at no time did our angel cry.

The lobby was empty that night, the T.V. was very loud, and one lone nurse sat at the front desk behind thick plexiglass. Both of us stood quietly in the lobby, hesitant to approach him. He looked up long enough to acknowledge that we were in the room before looking back at his magazine.

Janice walked closer to the front desk with the baby girl in her arms.

She was shaking, so I moved closer to comfort her.

"Excuse me," Janice said.

"Can I help you?" the nurse asked, looking up at us, then at the baby.

Janice didn't say anything. She stood frozen.

"Hello?" the nurse urged, with an aggravated tone. "Can I help you?"

I stepped in front of Janice and looked at his name tag, which read Mr. Allen.

"Mr. Allen, we need..." As I started to speak, our angel started to cry. She hadn't cried the entire time she had been with us or on the cold walk to the hospital. Her cry became more intense, and I knew right then we couldn't leave her there.

"Never mind," I said, turning to leave. Janice was out the door before I turned around.

As we hurried home, she stopped crying, which told me she wanted to stay with us. We decided to do our best to keep her safe, fed, and happy.

Chapter 2- John and Jorie

"I'll be up to bed in a minute. I want to finish the news," I yelled up the stairs to my husband, John. I'm sure he didn't hear me; he was probably already asleep. Watching the late-night news alone had become my entertainment, and that was a sad reality. I needed to find more things to do since John was gone every day and I was a housewife.

"The kitchen could use some tending to," I thought as the news came to an even less exciting end than the night before. I was thinking of anything to keep me from going up the stairs to bed and staring at the ceiling all night.

"I thought you were coming to bed after the news," John said from the last step of the stairs.

"Shoot, John! You scared me!"

"You promised you would try to sleep better, and this doesn't look like sleeping better to me," he said as he walked into the kitchen and turned off the light.

"I'm coming up now. I promise."

His eyes were tired, and he was not smiling.

"I promise," I pleaded, and he turned and walked slowly back up the stairs.

John and I have been together since high school. I graduated one year before him and started working at the post office. As soon as John graduated, we got married. Then, he went to college out of state on a football scholarship. We only saw each other when he would come home for winter, spring, or summer break. Everyone said we were too young to get married. I was 19 years old, and he was 18, but that didn't stop us. He told everyone who would listen that I was the only girl he ever looked at. I was an only child, and he had one sister. When he graduated from college, we planned to have a house full of children and live a simple life.

I listened for the door to the bedroom to close as I defiantly sat back on the couch. My journal was staring at me from the coffee table, and I knew it had been far too many days since I had written in it.

"Maybe writing will make me sleepy," I thought as I grabbed my journal and a pen:

December 18, 1993

Dear Journal,

Therapy doesn't seem to be working for me, and John seems to tire of my complaints. I am sure that if you could speak, you would say, "I am tired of you complaining, too." I go to sleep each night, anticipating waking up the following day with a renewed energy for life, but it doesn't seem to happen. This last miscarriage has taken my will to thrive.

My days seem to repeat on a wheel, similar to the life of a gerbil running in circles. I pray and meditate. I speak life, but nothing changes. I can close by saying that my faith is shaken but not dead. **-Jorie**

Chapter 3 – Hard Choices

"We can't keep letting her live like this, Stitch," Janice called out to me from the kitchen.

"I know! I know!" I yelled back at her.

"You say that, but it's been a year, and you ain't done nothing to get her a real home! This child doesn't even have a name!" Janice barked back at me.

I looked at our angel, wearing the stolen clothes too big for her. I knew she needed more, but I wasn't ready to let her go.

"Papa Stitch, eat," her little voice whispered.

I looked at her and smiled, groaning as I pulled myself off the floor to start what had become our morning ritual of eating hot cereal. After I prepared our little bowls, we ate on the floor together.

I spent the whole day watching her play. It was amazing. Within one year, she had grown a full head of silver curly locks to match her big round silver eyes that seemed to be able to see straight through me. I knew she was talking better than most babies her age. It just seemed as if she understood things.

The next evening, I told Janice that I had found a home for our angel, and it was time to say goodbye. Even though she didn't show it much, Jan had grown fond of having this little girl around. We had turned into a family.

After the streets went dark and quiet, I bundled up my little angel and strapped her into an old car seat I found one day. We then started walking in the direction of her new home. It was a freezing night, so Janice made sure to dress her warmly. Jan wanted to go with us, but I assured her that it was best that I go alone. I knew the walk to her new home would be hard because I could feel my heart breaking, and I didn't want to let Janice see me cry. I knew she would cry alone as soon as we left.

The house was only a few blocks away, even though it felt like we were walking for miles. When I reached the last corner, I looked to my right at the big house three doors down. All the lights were off, so I took a deep breath and walked towards it. I gently placed the tattered and worn car seat on the porch next to the front door.

"Well, this is it, my little angel," I smiled at her. As always, her eyes were wide and full of life. Despite the temperature and the tears in my eyes, she didn't cry or make a fuss.

I leaned over and whispered in her ear, "This is as far as Mr. Stitch can take you. These folks here are good, and I know they will take good care of you."

I didn't try to keep the tears from rolling down my face. "I love you, and thank you for choosing me."

As she smiled back at me, I knew she would be ok. I knocked on the door and waited until I heard someone moving around, then ran off.

Chapter 4 – Second Chances

"John! Wake up, someone's at the door," I whispered.

Startled, John woke up and immediately reached for his gun in the nightstand drawer.

"Why do you need your gun?" I asked nervously.

"Jorie, there's someone at the door, and it's 2 a.m. What do you think I need a gun for?" he whispered back in a groggy voice.

We got out of bed and started down the stairs. I followed a few steps behind him, with my heart beating rapidly.

"Who is it?" John yelled from the middle of the stairs. No answer.

"Who is it?" he yelled again louder, but no one answered. He tiptoed closer to the front door and pulled back the curtains slightly to get a better look. Just then, he saw a glimpse of a shadow running down the street. John opened the door quickly, firearm in hand, but the person was gone.

"It's too cold to be playing games at 2 a.m.," John said, frustrated, returning to the house.

"John, look!" I shrieked loudly, covering my mouth with both hands.

My heartbeat sped up.

"It's a baby! Someone left a baby!" I said, tapping his shoulder and pointing at the old car seat. I stepped before John and bent down to get a better look. It was a beautiful baby girl with silver hair and eyes looking up at me. I opened the blanket she was wrapped in just a little and noticed a note attached to her that read:

"Please take care of this little angel. She is very special."

We picked up the car seat and took her inside out of the cold. I stared at her for at least an hour before I could speak. John stared at me.

"What do you think we should do?" I finally asked. John paused and let out a long sigh. He knew how much I wanted a baby, but he didn't want me to be hurt again. After three miscarriages and adoptions that fell through, I don't think I could handle another disappointment.

He came over and sat next to me.

"Babe, it's completely up to you."

"This has to be a blessing for us, right?" I asked him. "Because what kind of cruel trick could this be?" By now, I was shaking on the inside.

"Yes." John nodded as he took me into his arms and held me tight. "This is the blessing we have been waiting for."

Chapter 5 – A Real Family

The next day, we took the baby to Child Protective Services and informed them of what happened. We also told them that we wanted to adopt her. This began some of the best and scariest months of my life. Each day came with its own emotion. We started a long process of filling out tedious paperwork and getting our home checked to be her foster parents. Then, we completed even more tedious paperwork and questionnaires to begin the adoption process. I answered each question with a mix of excitement and anxiety. I loved taking care of her and was eager to be her mom. But then doubt would come in, and I'd ask myself if I was ready for this and why. Why did she end up on my front porch?

Sometimes, after I put her down to sleep, I cried, thinking I had answered every question wrong and she would be taken away.

"They're going to think I'm unfit to care for her!" I cried to John.

"You're the only person fit to care for her," he assured me each time.

After 3 months, I had fallen into a routine of caring for her and her daily responsibilities, although she required very little. It was almost like she didn't need anything at all. I needed her more than she needed me.

The adoption court date had finally arrived on June 13th. "Are you OK?" John asked me. My face, as always, could not hide my feelings. I sat face-front and upright on the hard wooden bench in the courthouse lobby.

"John, if you ask me that again, I won't be ok!"

"Sorry," he said, nervously tapping his foot, bouncing his knee, and staring at the clock on the wall as each hour came and went. We were very nervous.

"Cookie, please?" the sweet voice called out from the stroller. The sound of her voice made me relax.

" You're awake?" I looked down into her bright silver eyes and smiled at her. "Are you hungry?" I asked while reaching into my overstocked baby bag for her cookies.

I stared at the tiny wonder as she quietly ate and looked curiously around the room.

"Parents, Jorie and John Price and infant child Mia Price," an elderly woman called out from behind the window. "You can come back now."

The sound of her name being called made my heart flutter with love. John allowed me the sole responsibility of choosing her name. I chose the name Mia. I genuinely believe I had spoken to her in existence with daily *I AM* statements. Each night, even in my darkest moments, I affirmed, "*I AM* a mother." She is proof of speaking life into what you desire.

"We are almost there, Mia," I told her. They're calling our name, baby girl. She laughed with excitement as if she knew what I was saying.

"I am ready to be the greatest mother to this beautiful little girl that The Universe has brought to us!" I said as we followed the clerk down the hallway.

After watching far too many television shows, the court area looked nothing like I thought it would. When I entered the small conference room, my vision of a white man in a robe and a lady sitting with a stenographer machine was erased.

As we pushed the stroller in, a county lawyer, one for the birth mother, and a social worker talked amongst themselves around a long wooden table. The magistrate entered the room, and eventually, the chatter at the table stopped. The conversation was directed toward us as we sat with our attorney and the Guardian Ad Litem.

"Thank you for your patience, Mr. and Mrs. Price," the judge said. "I know today has been long, and you are ready for this to all be over."

"Yes, Your Honor," our attorney responded quickly. John squeezed my hand under the table.

"We have made every attempt to find and contact the biological parents of the infant child, Mia. However, we have not been able to do so," said the attorney for the county. I breathed a sigh of relief.

"It is with the decision of the court to proceed with permanent custody and to move forward with the adoption of Mia Price to Mr. and Mrs. Price."

John lay his head on the wooden table and cried freely. "Thank you," John sniffled without looking up. This is all we ever wanted." I think he cried for me, too. I was overjoyed!

"I know she will be in good hands," the magistrate said as he smiled at us before standing and leaving. Mia kicked playfully in her stroller as everyone shook hands and left the room. We left the courthouse feeling the happiness we had wanted for a long time. We finally had a child of our own.

Chapter 6 –The Rare DNA

I believe I was more excited about the birthday party than Mia was. She was turning 3 years old, and this was her first birthday party with us as parents. The date was made up because we didn't know when she was born. So, we gave her a summer birthdate of June 25th, the same day my mother was born, and only 12 days after that date, we became an official family.

"Do you think you have enough balloons?" John laughed from the kitchen door.

I shot him a sarcastic look. "We can never have enough balloons for our Mia!"

"Clearly!" he laughed loudly. "But did we need the pony?" We both laughed together.

We held back nothing for this party. It was one of the things John and I had dreamed about doing for years. I didn't have much family I kept in touch with, so the party was filled with neighbors and John's family. Everything went better than planned, and Mia had the time of her life from the beginning to the end.

John walked the last guest out the door by 6 p.m. while I cleaned plates, cups, and trash. The gift table was filled with unopened presents and cards because Mia was too exhausted to open them and had fallen asleep on the couch.

"Awe, she is all partied out," I laughed. Admiring her resting so soundly made me take a moment to rest on the other end of the couch while John continued to clean.

****

"Jorie," John called out. "Are you coming to bed?"

His voice startled me. I didn't realize that I had dozed off to sleep. I looked over and saw Mia still sleeping, too.

"Yes, I'm coming up now. Let me get Mia."

"You're all partied out, I see," I whispered in her ear. As I picked her up from the couch, I softly ran my hand over her thick silver curly locks and kissed her head lightly. Immediately, I noticed the warmth on her forehead. As I put the back of my hand on her forehead, I saw the tiny

41

beads of sweat on her nose and that she was breathing fast.

"John..."

"Yes?" he answered back.

"John, something's wrong. She's breathing fast, and she's very hot."

I ran to the cabinet with her in my arms to get the digital thermometer. Her temperature read 106 degrees.

"Mia," I called her name softly and stroked her forehead. "Wake up, baby." Her eyes raced under her eyelids, but she did not respond.

"Get the car, John!" I screamed. "She's not waking up!"

"Calm yourself, Jorie, she's fine," I told myself as I continued to call her name and tap her shoulder. She did not respond.

The drive to the hospital seemed to take forever, but thankfully, it was only 2 miles away. The car barely came to a complete stop in front of the Emergency Room doors before I jumped out and ran inside with Mia limp in my arms. The lights in the ER lobby were bright and blinding.

"Help me, she's not waking up!" I said to the first person I saw. "Please help my baby!"

The nurses took us back immediately and started to work on her. They took her temperature, blood pressure, and oxygen while

John and I sat in the hard plastic chairs and watched helplessly. Mia lay unresponsive as they attached her to some machines. John held my hand tightly because he knew I needed it.

Nurses had come and gone for over two hours, and there were still no answers. We waited for the curtain to move or for a doctor to come in and give an update. I looked up at the clock. The time read 11:11 p.m.

"Can I have a cookie, please?" a little voice called out.

I jumped up immediately at the sound of her sweet voice. "Call the nurse, she's awake!"

For the next hour, multiple doctors came and went. They examined her body and drew blood samples while monitoring her heart, temperature, and blood pressure. They looked as confused as we felt. I no longer cared about what caused it. All that mattered was that Mia was awake. She was sitting in the bed watching them come and go as if nothing had happened. Her temperature was back to normal, and her eyes were wide open. Just as suddenly as *it* came, *it* went away. John was equally relieved yet still concerned at what had brought such a dramatic turn of her health. The doctors agreed it was a concern and decided to keep her overnight for observation. They were still waiting on test results. I encouraged John to go home and rest, but he refused to leave us. The nurses gave us a couple of blue hospital blankets, and we made ourselves comfortable in the chairs. We were not leaving her side tonight.

I was looking forward to taking Mia home and putting this nightmare behind us. Finally, a new doctor walked in and interrupted my thoughts. The look on his face made me wake John.

"What's wrong?" John and I asked simultaneously. The doctor could not hide his concern.

"I'm Dr. Sekou. I work primarily in the lab," he said calmly, despite the concern on his face.

"We received some of your daughter's test results and found an unknown DNA variation, and we would like to do more testing," he said.

"What do you mean by unknown?" John asked. "Is she okay?"

"Yes, she is physically okay and can go home. The fever is gone, and her blood pressure is normal. However, one of the blood tests came back abnormal, so we sent it out for further evaluation," he explained.

"There's something you're not saying, Doc," John interrupted. "Tell us what's wrong!"

"We sent your daughter's test to an independent lab," Dr. Sekou continued. "The test completed, called a GET -Gene Expression Test, found an unknown DNA sequence. This means the lab has no record of ever seeing DNA like hers.

We believe it may have been an error, so we resubmitted her blood to be tested again. We would also like to test both of you to get some answers. Does anyone else in your family have eyes like hers?" the doctor asked.

"We're not her biological parents. We adopted Mia," John said, looking helpless as he answered.

"Okay, I understand," the doctor responded. Is there any way to locate the biological mother or father?"

"No!" I answered quickly. "She abandoned her and never came back!"

John squeezed my hand. "It's alright, sweetie. He's just trying to help."

"I'm sorry. I didn't mean to upset you," Dr. Sekou said. "We will work with what we have and update you when the results come in."

"Thank you," John said to him as he walked out the door.

John and I moved around the small hospital room helplessly as we collected our things to leave. We were both unsure of how to feel. I looked over at Mia, who was calm as usual. She was fixated on a children's movie playing on the T.V. Before I knew it, tears were flowing from my eyes. Mia looked up and turned to me. "Mommy, it's going to be okay," she said, then smiled at me and turned back to look at the television. John and I stared at one another in shock.

Chapter 7- Reunited

(2 Years Later)

The first day of kindergarten was quickly approaching, and I was not ready. I was nervous about sending Mia to school and had to prepare myself to be brave. She had been home with us since the night she appeared on our porch. John and I agreed that daycare was not an option, especially after her hospitalization. Due to that incident, we feared leaving her unattended.

Two years had passed since the hospital visit, and no new incidents existed. She never had a cold, but we still wanted to be cautious. The second blood sample came back with the same results: that she had an unknown DNA sequence. The doctors didn't know what it was, how it was associated with her fever, or what to do. Since she seemed perfectly healthy, they only advised that we watch her for any changes.

Keeping her home had been effortless. She made parenting easy for me. She was an easy child to care for. She played alone for hours, and I would listen to her talk with her make-believe friends over the monitor. I was constantly amazed at how often Mia seemed to be able to solve her problems without my help, including calming herself down when things went wrong. I secretly wished I had the same abilities.

Mia and I practiced her first day of school routine, including getting on and off the bus all week.

"What number is your bus?" I asked her.

"Bus 606," she responded without looking up from playing.

"What do you do if you are not feeling well?"

"What's Mommy's number?"

"What's Daddy's number?"

She answered each question accurately, all while still playing.

****

"Today is the big day!" I said as we sat at the table. She smiled back at me while eating oatmeal, and her silver eyes beamed brightly. After she finished, Mia put her book bag on, just like we practiced, and stood at the kitchen door waiting for the bus to arrive. She stared out the window until the bus squealed to a stop at the street curb and then ran out. I watched from the kitchen doorway as she excitedly waited for the bus door to open. I could see that the driver was an older gentleman with gray wiry hair and a scruffy beard. He opened the door to let her in, but Mia paused and looked back at me briefly.

"Go ahead, Mia, just like we practiced," I said while smiling at her.

She turned back but did not move to get on the bus.

"I called back out to her. "It's ok to get on the bus, baby." My voice began to quiver, and I cleared my throat. I knew I had to hold it together for her. She looked back at me one last time, smiled, and waved goodbye as she stepped onto the bus. Relieved, I waved back.

"Good morning, Mr. Stitch."

"Good morning," he said.

Mia hopped onto her seat at the front, directly behind the driver.

The driver tried not to show his emotions. He couldn't believe that Mia had remembered him.

Mia leaned around the tall green seat. "I'm glad you're all better, Mr. Stitch," she said, smiling at him.

Chapter 8 – My Little Angel

"How could she have remembered me?" I wondered. I knew it was my little angel when I saw her silver eyes and curly silver hair walk up to the bus this morning. All day, I reminisced about the year she had lived with me and thought about the night I had dropped her off at that big house. That night, I knew I could never go back to the life I had been living before I found her. The next day, I took the first step and improved my life by going to the Veterans Hospital for help.

"Name and date of birth?" the case manager asked flatly through the clear plastic window.

"Bernard Randall, September 29, 1960."

"Address?" she asked without looking up.

"I'm homeless. I don't have an address."

I remember the questions seemed endless. I had to think long and hard about many of them because I had not had to answer to anyone since I was discharged from the service. I didn't know how tall I was or my weight. I didn't even know my hair color because I never looked in the mirror. I assumed it was gray.

"We have an open bed at the Salvation Army on 55th and Arlington near downtown. Can you get there, or will you need a bus ticket?"

"I will need a bus ticket, please," I answered.

"Please get there no later than 6 p.m. this evening, or you will not be admitted, and you will lose your bed," the case manager said, pushing the bus ticket under the plastic enclosure.

"I will be there. I have a promise to keep to myself." I remember being proud of myself as I stood to walk away despite others' doubts.

"Umm-hmmm," the case manager responded sarcastically, then called the next name in the lobby.

I sit in the bus behind the school in the parking depot, reflecting on how far I've come. I have not had a drop of alcohol since the night I found her. It has been a long journey, but I defeated the odds and have a house of my own to live in and a good job. I no longer steal or have to eat out of the trash. I've shared stories with my veteran buddies about the magical baby I found by a trash can and how looking into her eyes removed all the hurt I had been holding onto. None of them believed me, but I knew she had given me a new lease on life.

Chapter 9 – Mia

I couldn't wait to start kindergarten. Even though I had fun with Mommy, going to school would be the first time I saw new people and other kids daily. I was excited to go to school on the first day and even more excited when I saw Mr. Stitch as the bus driver. I missed him.

My new teacher's name was Ms. Bradley, and only 15 other kids were in her classroom. I made friends quickly, and everyone asked me questions about my hair and eyes. By the end of the day, every kid knew my name. "Mia, the girl with the sparkly eyes," they said.

Ms. Bradley wrote a special note for me to take home after the first day.

"Mia is a beautiful addition to our classroom. She is a little magnet of positive energy."

I was happy that Mommy was excited whenever I came home. She would talk about her day. She spoke so much that I fell asleep and didn't wake up until later that night. I even slept right through dinner.

The next few weeks were so much fun. I got to see Mr. Stitch, my new friends, color, and play on the playground. But I would always be tired when I came home. Mommy started having dinner ready when I got home so I could eat before falling asleep. Most afternoons, I wouldn't be hungry, just tired. I could feel it was bothering Mommy, but I couldn't help it. I overheard her talking to my auntie and Daddy about it on the phone.

"She's sleeping so much," I heard Mommy say. "This feels like the hospital incident, and Dr. Sekou's voice keeps chiming in the back of my head. What if something is wrong? Maybe we should keep her home."

Daddy was concerned, too, but I think he was more worried about Mommy. "She's just tired, Jorie. It's normal," he told her.

I didn't want her to worry either, but I didn't want her to keep me home. I liked school. I had lots of friends and had so much fun.

I remember the day things got strange. It was our first school assembly of the year, and all the other kids from K-5th grade got to be in the cafeteria together. I was super excited. We didn't see the big kids too much, and I had never been around so many kids at once. That day, I became the line leader and followed behind Ms. Bradley. We all sat at the cafeteria tables with the other classes, wiggling and giggling while we listened to the principal talk about all the stuff going on in school for this year. I didn't understand what he was saying until he mentioned that we were having a carnival in the fall with a petting zoo. All the kids screamed with excitement. I just quietly watched everyone. It was so amazing! Soon, I could feel myself getting tired, and I yawned a lot. Ms. Bradley looked at me and smiled.

"You didn't get enough sleep last night, Mia?"

I smiled back and continued listening to the principal. I started yawning again and was so sleepy that I put my head on the table and closed my eyes.

****

"Mia," Ms. Bradley called out. I could hear her, but I couldn't answer her.

"I don't think she feels good," said a boy from my class. "She put her head down a long time ago."

"Mia." Ms. Bradley tapped my arm gently. "It's time to go, sweetie."

I still couldn't answer, although I could hear her. The assembly must have been over.

Ms. Bradley moved closer and noticed my breathing was very short and quick. "Mia," she whispered as she signaled for another teacher to help.

"Please tell the principal I need help," she told the teacher.

"And please take the other students back to the classroom," she told her teacher's assistant. The nurse, who was also in the cafeteria, rushed over immediately.

I could feel Ms. Bradley's heartbeat getting faster, and her voice was shaking. I wanted to tell her I was ok and was just tired, but I couldn't speak.

"She's burning up," I heard the nurse say after touching my forehead. The nurse pulled her thermometer out of her jacket pocket. "Her temperature is 107," she said. "Call the parents and have them meet us at the hospital."

Chapter 10 - Who I Am

The school's phone number was displayed on the caller ID, and my heart skipped a beat as I answered. "107-degree temperature" and "meet at the hospital" were all I heard the school nurse say.

"I'm on my way!" I said, disconnecting and calling John.

"It's happening again, John!" I screamed. "She won't wake up!"

I jumped into the car and drove down the street erratically, with so many thoughts going through my mind. I could barely focus on the road. My mind was in a fog.

Here we were again, sitting in the Emergency Room. It felt like a nightmare, and I couldn't wake up.

I arrived at the hospital before John. Everything went in the same order: nurses, doctors, examinations, and tests. And just like last time, they couldn't determine what was wrong. John arrived, and we waited for hours before he and I fell asleep in the hard, uncomfortable chairs while Mia slept in the hospital bed.

Mia awakened me and the nurse's light-hearted giggling as Mia tried to share her graham crackers and juice with her. Just then, John walked in with two cups of coffee.

"She woke up a little after 11 p.m.," the nurse told us as she finished taking Mia's vitals. The ER doctor walked into the room and gave us a thumbs-up sign. She smiled and told us that her test results were normal and that there was no damage to her heart, brain, or kidneys.

"Just as before, it's a miracle and a mystery," the doctor stated as she turned to walk away.

"Wait a minute!" I responded angrily. "What do you mean? This is not normal!" I said, growing frustrated. "We need some answers. We can't keep going through this, hoping next time won't kill her!"

"I apologize for being so casual," the doctor said. "I meant that she is out of any immediate danger. Her temperature is normal, and she is cleared for discharge in the morning. Dr. Sekou will come talk to you in a few minutes."

We waited patiently until Dr. Sekou came into the room. "Have there been any changes in her routine recently?" Dr. Sekou asked while pulling out a notebook and pen.

"Not much," I responded. "She has been doing so well for the past couple of years. We thought what happened before must have been a one-time situation. She started kindergarten about a month ago and has been sleeping a lot lately after school," I told him. "We just figured she was tired from a long day."

"Would it be ok if I looked further into this?" he asked.

"Of course!" We responded together.

"This has been so stressful. We don't know what is happening or how to help her," John continued.

"I would like to see her in a few weeks at my private practice," he said, handing John a card with the appointment information.

The next day, Mia was discharged, and we were happy to leave together. John pulled the car around to the ER entrance, and Mia and I got in. She played quietly in the back seat as John, and I exchanged glances of concern but rode home in silence.

We decided it best that Mia stay home from school the rest of the week so we could keep an eye on her. Like in the previous episode, she showed no new symptoms, and her sleep pattern was normal.

The week passed, and I looked forward to the weekend. Saturday morning was always laid-back because John was off from work. Mia was eating oatmeal on the carpet in front of the television.

"Ding-dong," the doorbell rang.

"John, are you expecting anyone?" I called out.

"It's Mr. Stitch, Mommy," Mia answered without looking away from the television.

I walked into the living room from the kitchen, a bit confused.

"How do you know who is at the door?" I asked her.

"I don't know," she shrugged. "I can feel him."

I walked slowly towards the door, moving the thick curtains to the side to look through the large window. There stood the bus driver on our front porch—Mr. Stitch, just as Mia said.

"John, come here!" I called out again whlle opening the door.

"Good morning, Mr. Stitch. This is a surprise. What brings you here?"

"Mia, ma'am," he stuttered. "I kept hearing her voice in my head, telling me to come over and tell you what I know."

"You heard Mia's voice in your head?" I asked him, looking for John to come down the stairs.

"Yes, ma'am. I heard Mia's voice," he said. "I can't explain how."

I turned to look at Mia, but she was still watching cartoons.

"Come in; my husband will be down in a moment. Can I get you something to drink?"

"Yes, please, and thank you," he replied.

My hands shook as I reached for a glass in the kitchen cabinet. I made him some ice water and walked back into the living room just as John entered.

"What's going on?" John said as he walked in. "Why is the bus driver here?"

"He said Mia told him to come," I answered, raising my eyebrows suspiciously.

"You're saying that our 5-year-old daughter told you to come over here?" John asked him in a condescending tone. "And how did she do that?"

"Sir, I know this sounds crazy, but I initially ignored it, figuring I was having a senior moment or something. For the past few days, I heard her voice inside my head, telling me to come here and tell you the truth. The more I ignored it, the louder it got. So that's why I'm here," he said, lifting the glass to his lips with his hands shaking as well.

"That doesn't make any sense," John said, throwing his hands up.

Mia got up from the floor and took her bowl to the kitchen. Then she walked over to her daddy.

"It's okay, Daddy. I asked him to come over to tell you what he knows."

John and I looked at each other in disbelief.

"How did you call him?" I asked her.

"With my mind," she said, walking over to Mr. Stitch and looking him in the eyes.

"Please tell them what you know so they won't worry about me."

"But I don't know much," he responded, looking into her bright silver eyes.

"It's okay; just tell them the truth. They will understand," Mia said and went back to watching television.

John and I were curious and afraid about what he had to say. We all walked into the living room to sit down and hear him out.

Mr. Stitch placed his glass on the coffee table and said, "I used to be homeless. I found Mia wrapped up near a trash can in the bitter cold about five years ago. It was nothing short of a miracle that she was still alive because it was so cold outside. Janice and I, my lady then, asked around to find out who had recently been pregnant in the area. Eventually, we found out that a homeless girl named Honesty had been pregnant, and then she wasn't, but nobody saw her with a baby. Honesty was known to be in the streets, living in a bad kind of way. She was known to use a lot of different drugs. Pretty much anything she could get her hands on. We looked all over but couldn't find her. The word on the streets was that she had left the area.

"Janice and I were trying to do the right thing by keeping Mia with us. She didn't even have a name, but I called her my little angel. I didn't take her to Child Protective Services because I was scared that she would end up with a bad foster family like I experienced when I was a child. We took care of her as best we could. We were squatting in an old abandoned house not too far from here. I was able to get the power on and get us some heat, but it wasn't enough. I'm ashamed to say that what we couldn't find in the trash bins, I stole to keep my little angel clothed and fed. By the time she started crawling and talking, we knew she needed better." Stitch wiped his eyes at the thought, sadly looking down.

"I have been walking these streets for a long time and have seen y'all many times. You and your husband always seemed to be so nice to one another. You were always kind to me. You never treated me mean if I walked by here. One day, I saw you sitting on your porch crying, ma'am. I heard you talking about losing your baby. So, when it was time to find her a good home, I remembered you. I knew this was where I had to bring Mia. I knew she would be safe, and you would love her like she needed to be loved. So yes, I'm the one who brought her over here and left her on your porch. "But ma'am and sir, that's about all I know," he said, lifting his hands.

"This can't be real," John said, resting his face in his hands.

"I have been thinking the same thing," Stitch said. "I knew it was her when I stopped at your house on the first day of school and saw her curly silver hair, but I was shocked that Mia recognized me when she got on the bus. She sat behind me and told me she was glad I was all better. How could she have remembered me from when she was a baby? How could she have known that I had gotten help?"

Stitch got up to leave.

"I'm sorry for all the confusion, Mr. Stitch," I said as we walked towards the door.

"I just wanted her to be safe and be with good people," he said.

I looked over at Mia, who was still watching cartoons.

"Please don't apologize," I said to him.

"Thank you so much for choosing us. She has been the light we needed!"

"Yes, ma'am," Stitch responded. "She saved my life. She gave me a reason to live. This was the first decision I made in a long time that turned out good!" he said, wiping the tears that ran down his face from his tired eyes.

"It's okay now, Mr. Stitch," said Mia. "You helped them to know who I am." She stood up from her seat on the floor and hugged him.

Chapter 11 – Superior Sensitive Processing

The next few weeks consisted of several tests for Mia. We drove back and forth to Dr. Sekou's office at least two to three times a week. I was drained from the whole process, but Mia had been a trooper. She was a little upset about missing school and her friends, but we thought it best that she stayed home until we could return to our regular daily schedule.

On Friday morning, when we didn't have anything scheduled with Dr. Sekou, he called to give us some information but did not want to discuss it over the phone. I immediately called John.

****

John and I waited in the lobby
of Dr. Sekou's office with Mia. The
space was narrow, with four wooden
chairs, a coffee table filled with
magazines, and a tall artificial Ficus
tree that needed dusting. Dr. Sekou's
secretary, a gray-haired Asian
woman, spoke loudly on the phone
from behind the sliding glass
receptionist window.

"Mr. and Mrs. Price, Dr. Sekou will
see you now," the secretary said
pleasantly, then slid the window
closed again. John and I looked at one
another. "We got this!" he said. We
walked hand in hand with Mia in the
middle, down the short corridor to
his office.

Much like the lobby, the office was outdated and small. But as we entered, it felt relaxing. He had eclectic art on the walls, several living plants, African sculptures on the bookshelves, and a soothing water fountain rockery stream on his desk.

Dr. Sekou was scribbling in his notebook quickly, looking up long enough to say, "Please close the door behind you." Then he looked back at his notes for a bit longer as we sat on the leather couch with Mia nestled between us.

After a moment, he gave us his attention and began to speak.

Mr. and Mrs. Price, "Your daughter has what is known as SSP—Superior Sensitive Processing. She is highly sensitive to external and internal stimuli. I also performed a CNS, which measures cognitive neurosensitivity, and I detected high cognitive processing with abnormal brain activity."

"That's a lot of big words, Doc. What does that mean?" John asked.

Dr. Sekou looked at us. "Do you recall when she was in the hospital before and the GET -Gene Expression Test came back with an unknown DNA sequence?"

"Yes," we both answered.

"The tests I ran at my private practice have identified the sequence. It means that Mia can feel other people's feelings, hear things most people can't hear, and see things most people can't. But more importantly, the reason I asked to test her further and outside the hospital was because her blood work is very similar to that of another child that was admitted to the hospital some time ago," he continued.

"The boy, Jamil X, was brought into the ER with similar symptoms to Mia. He had an extremely high temperature, fast breathing, and was in a deep sleep that no one could wake him up from. While we were testing him, he suddenly woke up as if nothing was wrong, just like Mia. He was in foster care, and the foster parents told us that he would sleep for hours, eventually waking and returning to normal. The foster parents said Jamil was powerful for a 5-year-old, and he told his foster parents that he could hear people's thoughts. Of course, they assumed he was hallucinating.

"His medical history showed he was born to a parent addicted to drugs. I was unable to follow up with his foster parents about the blood results I sent to the independent lab because he was moved to a new foster home and seemed to disappear from the system. I tried to find him, but I was unsuccessful. No one I talked to at CPS ever saw him again."

We explained to Dr. Sekou the story Mr. Stitch told us about how he found Mia and who he believed to be her mother. I told him how Mr. Stitch said he had heard Mia's voice in his head, and she had asked him to come to our house and explain what he knew about her and her biological parents.

Dr. Sekou looked surprised. "Jamil X and Mia's blood results are very similar. You can tell no one about these test results or her abilities," he strongly advised.

Mia giggled because John's knee was bouncing so vigorously from nervousness.

"Daddy, you're gonna make me fall," she laughed.

"Oh, I'm so sorry, baby," John replied.

It's okay, you're scared," Mia said. "Mommy is scared, too."

The room was silent as we all looked at her.

"Dr. Sekou, what does this mean? Is Mia in danger?" I asked him.

"If you want to keep her safe, do not tell anyone about her abilities. We should meet elsewhere after today," he stated as we stood to leave. "I will be in touch."

We were shaken up as we walked out into the corridor.

"Remember to tell no one!" Dr. Sekou whispered outside the door.

John and I did not speak as we rode home, and Mia played with her doll in the back seat. We were terrified, not wanting to talk to family or friends for fear of being deemed crazy or someone leaking our information.

We put Mia to bed early that evening, which gave John and me time to discuss the doctor's report.

"What do you think about all of this?" I asked him as he stoically stared at the television.

"I don't know what to think. This is a lot to process," John said. "Is he saying our baby is psychic? Has powers?" he asked, dropping his head into his hands and rubbing his temples.

"I don't know what to think either," I responded.

I guess there was nothing he or I could say or do. We had to wait for the next meeting with Dr. Sekou. Mia returned to school the following

Monday, and we fell into our regular routines.

After a few weeks, as John and I watched the late-night news, a picture of Dr. Sekou flashed onto the screen.

"The Cleveland Police have issued a missing person alert for 41-year-old Dr. Sekou, who was last seen at his private practice. His wife reported him missing after he did not return home last night."

John and I looked at each other in fear. Without saying a word, we knew something was wrong, and we needed to leave town tonight.

"Pack what you can," John said. "We will buy what we need when we get there."

****

Our lives changed in a matter of minutes the night Dr. Sekou went missing. We packed four large suitcases filled with all the clothes and personal items that could fit. I packed a few boxes of pictures and memorabilia, all of Mia's clothes, and a few of her favorite toys. We loaded up our van, strapped Mia in her car seat, and left our home in the middle of the night. I had never felt so afraid.

We drove all night. I looked in the rearview mirror over 100 times until we were out of Ohio. Once we felt safe enough to stop, we checked into a hotel, and John called some of his old college friends. Within a few calls, he had a new job, and we had a new place to live without any questions being asked. We didn't want his parents to worry, so we told them that John had a great opportunity and we had to move quickly. We didn't dare risk telling anyone what Dr. Sekou told us. After we showered, rested, and fed Mia, we began our 30-hour journey to Moscow, Idaho, and never talked about Dr. Sekou again.

Chapter 12 - Being the Weird Girl

(7 Years Later)

The warm breeze from the open window felt good as I rode the bus for my first day of middle school. I sat in the first seat, right behind the bus driver, as I had done in Cleveland. Old memories instantly came flooding back. I remembered the last night we were in Cleveland and how we packed up and moved in the middle of the night. Mommy told me we were going on an adventure, but I knew it was because they were scared about what the doctor said and how he went missing. I could feel my mother's fears and hear her heart. It was beating so hard. I was disappointed that I didn't get to see Mr. Stitch one more time.

We had been living in Idaho for seven years, and finally, my parents were letting me go back to school. I was so excited. Not that I didn't love their company, but there were only so many manicures and pedicures Mommy and I could do together. And watching TV after work with Daddy didn't entirely replace having friends my age.

We lived almost 10 miles from town, and the closest neighbors lived a mile from our house, and they were younger than me. The house we moved to was much smaller than the one we had back in Ohio. We could probably fit our new home on the first floor of our old one. The yard was way bigger, though. I could run and jump, skip and run some more.

I was the first stop and the only kid on the bus until we picked up a group of kids a few miles away. I smiled as they entered the bus.

"Why is she smiling at everybody?" I heard one of the boys say as he walked past me on the bus.

"I don't know, but she looks like an old lady with all that gray hair!" I heard another boy say, laughing obnoxiously.

Just that fast the happiness of my first day back at school was quickly wiped away. Maybe sitting at the kitchen table and being homeschooled by Mommy wasn't a bad idea. I turned and faced the window in silence.

Going back to school was supposed to be a great experience. I was looking forward to meeting new kids and getting invited to sleepovers and birthday parties. Those kids will be at the school because they weren't on this bus. The bus driver was no Mr. Stitch either. He barely spoke to anyone.

Once the bus reached town, it filled up pretty fast. It felt like we were stopping every few minutes to let on more talkative pre-teens.

"Excuse me," I heard a voice call out. I continued looking out the window, watching the cars pass.

"Excuse me," the small voice spoke again. "Can I sit with you?"

I turned around to look and saw a small girl with narrow eyes, long dark hair, and a warm smile.

"Of course," I replied and smiled back at her.

"Thank you," she said. "My name is Natalia, but kids call me Tai mainly because they can't pronounce my name."

"Nice to meet you, Tai. My name is Mia."

Tai and I chatted for the remainder of the ride to school, making me feel much better. We soon discovered that we shared a few classes and had lunch at the same time. I was happy to have at least one new friend since the other kids only stared at me. The ones who talked to me just asked questions about my hair and eyes.

I sat with Tai at lunch, and we talked like we had known each other for years. We chatted about everything we had in common while picking over the cold sandwiches and stale chips that neither of us wanted.

It didn't take long for me to catch the attention of the school bullies. My head, full of curly silver hair and bright silver eyes, made me an easy target.

"I see the new weird girl has met the old weird girl," a chunky boy with bad acne and hair slicked back said. He laughed sarcastically as he approached our lunch table.

"You're funny, Tre," laughed the other boys with him.

Tre, short for Robert Louis III, was the school bully. He laughed loudly, causing more kids to look and see who he was picking on.

"I guess this gon' be the weird girl table," he said as he leaned over and stuck his finger in the middle of my sandwich.

"Please stop it," I heard my new friend Tai say in her small, soft, meek voice.

Tai was the only person who had been nice to me; now, she stood up for me.

"Or what?" Tre asked aggressively as he balled up my sandwich in his fist.

"Walk away, please," I said as calmly as possible. I kept my eyes focused on the lunch tray in front of me as my anger grew.

"Like I said, or what weirdo?" he asked again. He leaned in uncomfortably close to my face. So close I could smell his foul breath and musty body odor overpowering his cheap deodorant.

I felt my face warming up and my hands starting to tingle. I pushed my chair back to give myself room to breathe and stand up. My heart was beating fast. It felt like it was about to burst through my chest, and the heat in my head was becoming more intense as he continued to taunt me. Soon, we were surrounded by more students who came over to watch the antics.

"I told you to walk away!" I said again, this time with more force in my tone.

Not even I was prepared for what came next, as the room went dark. My eyes began to burn, and I could feel my heart racing like a horse inside my chest. I didn't know what was happening, and I felt angry.

I looked him directly in his eyes and whispered, "Eat your words."

His hands began to lift like robots, and he picked up the last pieces of the balled-up sandwich, smashing them into his face.

I could feel one of Tre's friends coming from behind me.

   "What did you do to Tre, you freak?" he yelled, reaching out to grab my shoulder.

I turned to him and whispered, "Keep your hands to yourself."

The boy began slapping himself across the face repeatedly.

"Now cry and show them what a coward you are," I said, staring at him. The boy began crying and ran from the cafeteria.

My eyes began to cool as I looked around the room, which had been buzzing with middle school noise but was now quiet. I could see the facial expressions of awe, fear, and confusion.

"What the hell did you do to me, you freak?" Tre asked in bewilderment as he wiped off his face.

"I asked you to stop, but I guess you didn't hear me," I said.

"What's going on over there?" the lunchroom monitor called out. All the kids scattered, whispering and pointing at me, but I didn't care.

"Woah!" Tai said in amazement as she walked off with the crowd.

"Yes!" I thought to myself with confidence. Everything I thought I could do in my mind, I can do for real! I always knew I had powers but didn't know how to use them.

****

The rest of the day continued without any more drama and the bus ride home wasn't as bad as the morning. I guess word got around about what happened in the cafeteria with Tre. When Tai got off at her stop, I was alone again. No one would talk to me, but I could hear their thoughts.

"She's kind of weird."

"She scares me."

"I don't want to look into those eyes."

Hearing other people's thoughts was nothing new to me. I recalled my friend Imani, who rode my bus when we were in kindergarten. Imani had red hair and freckles. Her clothes were always dirty, but I could feel she had a pure heart. She was shy, and we sat together every day.

Then, one day, she wasn't on the bus, and I didn't see her anymore. I was sad because I had no one to sit with, even though she didn't talk much.

A few nights after she stopped riding the bus, I heard her voice as I drifted off to sleep in my bedroom.

"I'm so sad they moved me again," she said.

I looked around my room, but she wasn't there.

"I tried to be good. They didn't want me anymore," she said, crying.

I ran to my parents' room so fast, screaming, "Someone is in my room, but I can't see them!"

They dismissed it as a bad dream, and Mommy took me back to bed and cuddled me until I fell asleep.

After that night, I didn't hear Imani's voice again.

I heard the neighbors' kids from a mile away. They sounded fun and energetic. I enjoyed listening to them because I had no one to play with. It made me feel like I was there.

But other times, I could hear the sad voices of children calling out for help. I tried to shut them out, but they were loud and clear. The frightened cries were real. Just like my own cry the night I was left alone after I was born.

It was the coldest night on record in the small city of Cleveland, Ohio. The temperature had fallen to -20 degrees Fahrenheit. I can remember the sound of the whistling winds, yet I don't remember feeling its chill. I remember the barren tree limbs that were frozen over with hanging icicles. They looked like decorations. I remember feeling as if there were no signs of life. No animals or humans, except me, a baby born and left to survive in the cold.

The bus finally pulled up to the last stop, which was my house. I lived the furthest out, so I was the first one on and the last one off. I grabbed my book bag and said, "See ya' later," to

the driver, glad to see the first day of
middle school in my rear-view mirror.

Chapter 13 - Transitions

The transition to Idaho seven years ago was hard for John and me, but we didn't think twice about getting Mia away from danger. If they snatched that doctor, there was no telling what they would have done to us.

We have an entirely different lifestyle now. Our three-story Victorian-style home in the city had been downsized to a small, three-bedroom, one-story ranch house on 5 acres. What we gave up in size, we gained in green grass, fresh air, and peace of mind. John got a job in sales that he hated because it kept him on the road more, leaving Mia and me home alone. I homeschooled for fear that someone would find out about her. She didn't have another episode, which kept us out of the emergency room and made us have to answer questions for which we had no explanations. Life was peaceful, and Mia became my entire world.

We celebrated our family adoption day and Mia's birthday with just the 3 of us. I knew Mia needed social interaction with other kids, but I feared letting her go too far. When she was younger, she sometimes played with the neighbor's children, a boy and a girl who lived about a mile away. But their family moved, and I had been apprehensive about finding her new playmates. I tried to keep Mia busy, but there wasn't much for a little girl to do in this town.

As the summer ended, John and I had a long discussion. We agreed that we felt safer here and that it was time to make changes. Mia would return to school, and I would get involved in the community. Mia was elated, and I looked forward to making new friends and having adult conversations again.

The first day of school came so fast. It was like the first day of kindergarten all over again. I was anxious, unlike Mia, who ran out the door at the sound of the bus pulling up. John had taken a few days off from work to be home with us for her first few days of school. I was a nervous wreck. Each time the phone rang, I knew it would be the school calling to say Mia was sick with a high fever.

"You can't worry about yourself like that all day," John said from the couch. "She will be fine. She has been doing great!"

I knew that he was right, and I shouldn't worry. She had been fine, except for one incident I never told him about. Thinking back on it now frightens me.

"Mia," I called, but she did not respond. I got up to look into her room and saw her lying motionless, sound asleep. I smiled and began to close the door, but something about how her arms were positioned straight down by her sides made me pause.

I called her name repeatedly, shaking her, but she would not wake up.

I ran to grab the thermometer and my cell phone from the nightstand by my bed. Her breathing remained steady, her eyes moved under the lids, and her temperature was normal. I didn't want to alarm John, so I took several deep breaths to relax. I decided to sit next to her and pray. An hour passed before she woke up talking strangely about going to save a little girl. I shook it off as a dream and never mentioned it again. However, my heart knew it was more than that.

The bus screeching to a stop snapped me out of my thoughts and brought me so much relief. I peeked out the window and saw Mia stepping off the bus. She made it home.

"Welcome home, baby!" I said, opening the door. "How was your day?"

"It was terrible!" she cried while throwing down her book bag.

"Oh no! What happened, baby girl?" John asked from his spot on the couch.

"The kids are mean, and they think I'm a freak!" she cried as she sat down next to John. We nestled her in the middle as we had done many times before.

"Mia, you are not a freak. You are individually made. You are here on purpose and for a purpose," I told her, hugging her tight.

"I know, that's what you always tell me, but some days I just want to be normal. I don't want to be weird. I don't want to have whatever this is that I have."

John and I looked at one another in surprise. "What do you have?" I asked.

"I hear people, I see people, and I feel people! This has been happening for as long as I can remember. I didn't want to scare you like I did with Mr. Stitch and Dr. Sekou."

"You remember that?" John asked.

"I remember everything, Daddy!" she cried out.

"Listen to me!" he said, placing her face in his palms.

"You saved our life the day you showed up on our porch. You also saved Mr. Stitch the moment you entered his life. We may not understand this gift and how it works, but I understand that you are here to help someone. Your beautiful silver eyes see things that no one else can see. Your silver hair has wisdom. You have this gift to do good in the world."

She looked up at us, eyes swollen and nose red. We were not used to seeing her cry. She had never let out this much emotion.

I took off the necklace that was around my neck.

"I bought this necklace 11 years ago. I was in a dark and sad place. John and I wanted to have children badly, but it didn't look like it would ever happen. I decided then that I needed to accept who and where I was in my life."

Mia wiped her eyes and looked at the turquoise necklace encased with three silver letters that read *I AM*.

"*I AM* are two of the most powerful words in the world. These words give you strength. Believing in who you are is the greatest power on Earth! I took these three letters and rearranged them to name you Mia. Every time I speak your name, it is an answered prayer. Wear this necklace and trust The Universe to reveal to you what your purpose is."

Mia wiped the tears from her cheeks, and John put the necklace around her neck. She smiled and lit up my heart once again. "Thank you, Mommy and Daddy. I needed to hear that."

We ordered a pizza and ate while Mia shared all she had been holding inside. She told us that she remembered the night Mr. Stitch found her. She shared that she could hear people's thoughts and feelings when going to the nail salon and the grocery store. I reminded her that she used to talk to imaginary friends, and she corrected me. She explained they weren't imaginary, but she was pretending to play with other children she could hear playing miles away.

"I can even hear kids that are very unhappy."

"What do you mean, Mia?" John asked.

"One night, I heard the voice of a girl calling out for help. I felt so confused. I closed my eyes tightly and lay very still. Then, peaceful energy came over me. Even though I didn't know what was happening, I kept my eyes closed and gave in to the feeling without fear. When I opened my eyes, I was somehow in a different house. It smelled of mold and rotting garbage. Then I felt a darkness. I started to feel afraid, but I told myself to be brave."

"Help me," she cried out to me.

"Where are you?" I whispered.

"I'm in the closet," she called out.

I walked over to the closet and opened it. A small girl with terrified eyes was dangling from a wall-mounted coat hook.

"Help me," she whimpered.

I smiled to give her comfort and lifted her slowly from the wall.

"How did you get stuck up there?" I asked.

"My new daddy," she said.

"She went on to tell me that her new foster parents were mean and would hang her on the hook in the closet when she was bad. My heart sank, and I became angry. I knew I had to get her out of there, but before I could say anything else, I woke up in bed with you staring at me, Mommy."

I was at a loss for words, recalling the night that I tried to wake her, and she wouldn't budge.

"We have to keep this quiet, Mia," John told her.

"I know," she responded, "because of what they did to that boy Jamil X."

"What do you know about Jamil?" we asked her simultaneously.

"I saw him in my mind that day at Dr. Sekou's office. Somebody took him and locked him up."

I was alarmed. We had not spoken of Dr. Sekou in 7 years, and now our daughter reveals that she has known everything and more all along.

"Well, it sounds like our daughter has superpowers!" John said, breaking up the tension. We all laughed and finished eating the pizza. But I knew this was serious, and things were about to change again.

Chapter 14 - I Use My Powers for Good

The next day, the bus ride to school was great. As Tai and I talked, it felt like a weight had been lifted off my shoulders. All of the years of having to keep things a secret were over. I was free to tell my parents everything. No more hiding what I truly felt. Mommy and I had always been close, but somehow this made us closer. They were still worried about me, so we promised to keep my powers a secret and only talk about them at home.

Tre told everyone how I made his mind do weird things. This brought on a mixture of reactions from the other students. Some were afraid, others were curious. No one admitted they believed him but chose not to test me, so they decided not to talk to me. There were no bullies, but there were no new friends either.

Tai became my best friend. We were inseparable. We liked the same things and talked on the phone every day after school. We were excited about the school dance that was coming up and couldn't wait to go.

Our mothers took us shopping to pick out cute outfits. We laughed and chatted in the backseat the entire ride to the shopping center.

"We should dress alike for the dance," Tai said. I laughed at the thought. We had many things in common, but our fashion styles weren't one of them. We walked into multiple stores and tried on different clothes we liked. And at the end of the shopping day, our outfits were utterly different. Tai chose a short floral dress with tan kitten heels to match. And I decided to rock a jacket with matching jeans and a pair of Jordans.

"You two are like yin and yang," Mommy said.

"Who?" Tai and I questioned each other at the same time.

Our moms laughed at us. I was happy to see my mom finding a friend as well.

****

Saturday was the night of the school dance, and I was nervous. I watched Mommy, equally anxious, running around the house looking for an outfit to wear to dinner with Tai's mom, Melissa.

"What about this dress?" she asked for the third time. "That's fine, too, Mommy!" I said, sitting on the couch, ready to go. "It's just dinner."

She laughed at herself. "You're right. It's been so long since I've been out with a friend that I don't know what to wear." She ultimately decided on the first outfit.

Melissa picked us up, and we rode to the dance together. Even though I was happy to see Tai, I couldn't shake my nervousness.

"We'll be a few minutes away in town if you need us," Mommy repeated as we approached the school.

"Stop! You're hurting me!" I heard a boy's voice call out. I turned to look around, but no one was there.

"We know, at Applebee's," Tai said as she kissed her mom on the cheek and hopped out of the van.

"We will be fine, Mommy. Y'all go have fun," I said as I quickly got out. Then I leaned into the passenger's side window and kissed her on the cheek before running off.

As soon as we walked into the hallway, I felt another, more intense feeling. This time, fear and panic rushed through my body like lightning. The feeling was so strong that I got light-headed. I paused and took a deep breath.

"It's crowded," Tai said, looking around at the fabulous decorations.

"Yeah, the whole school is here," I replied, trying to hide my uneasiness.

The music was loud, and a song Tai liked was playing. She raised her arms in a waving motion and started dancing.

"Get off of me! I can't breathe!" the boy's voice called out again, so loud I could hear it over the music. I turned around to look at Tai, who was still dancing. I wanted to ask her if she heard it too, even though I knew she hadn't.

"I'm in the bathroom! Hurry!" the boy cried out.

The music became lower in my ears, and I could feel the boy's panic and fear.

"I need to go to the bathroom. I will be right back," I told Tai, turning to leave the gym to walk down the hallway.

"Do you want me to go with you?" she asked, not missing a beat.

The panic came faster and harder. My walk turned into a run. Tai was behind me as I ran straight into the boy's bathroom without hesitation.

"Mia, you're going into the wrong bathroom. That's the boy's bathroom!" Tai called out. I continued in, coming face-to-face with three boys who had a small boy pinned to the ground. They were digging through his pockets and smashing his face to the floor. His wire-framed glasses were bent on his face, filled with tears.

"Get out of here!" the larger boy turned and shouted at me.

"Get off of him!" I said in a stern voice.

"Do you want some of this, too?" he asked mockingly. The other boys laughed, turning their attention to me as well.

"Get off of him now!" I repeated, clenching and releasing my hands.

"You can take his place, you freak," he said, rising from off the small boy's back.

My heart beat faster; my eyes began to burn. I clinched and released my hands rapidly.

"What the heck? Her eyes are turning colors!" one of the boys said.

"You will leave him alone," I heard myself say in a voice I didn't recognize.

I lifted my hand, and the large boy's arms dropped. His face went blank, and he stood up.

"Tell them to leave him alone!" I commanded, pointing at the other boys, still kneeling on the frail kid.

"Leave him alone! Leave him alone! Leave him alone!" the ringleader repeated repeatedly, in a robotic voice, each time getting louder.

The other boys looked confused as they stood up.

"Dude, why are you talking like that?"

The large boy continued chanting as the others stood up to run out the door.

"Dude, you're being weird! We're outta here!"

The boy picked himself up off the floor and adjusted his glasses. He wiped the tears from his eyes and walked towards the door. He turned around and looked back at the bully, who was still chanting. Then he looked at me in astonishment.

"Thanks," he said timidly. I did not respond.

The big bully continued chanting for a few more seconds before I lowered my hand and walked over to him, continuing to look into his eyes.

"You will not bother him or anyone else again," I whispered. He nodded his head like a programmed robot.

"Now go!" I commanded.

His eyes opened wide, and he looked around, confused.

"What happened? Where are my friends?" he asked before running out of the bathroom.

I turned to watch him leave and saw Tai standing in the doorway with her arms crossed, smirking.

"So you got some kind of superpower?" We both stared at one another quietly for a second.

"Yeah, kind of," I said shyly. "I shouldn't have done that in front of people. Promise you won't tell anyone."

"Well, I think it's pretty damn dope!" Tai said. "Your secret is safe with me, Mia Price. Just don't turn me into a frog or a pumpkin."

"I use my powers for good, but don't test me," I said, and we laughed. I let out a sigh, feeling less and less alone.

I knew I could trust Tai, and now I have my parents with whom I share my journey. We walked back to the gymnasium and partied together at our first dance. We had a great time!

Chapter 15 - Finding Our Voice

I suggested at the PTA meeting, "We can host a bake sale for Valentine's Day. The students can buy cupcakes or cookies to give to one another. We could also do a flower-gram."

"What is that?" Mrs. Grimes, the PTA secretary, asked.

"It's when students purchase a carnation for $1 and write a note to their friends. The carnations with the note attached will be delivered to the intended recipient's homeroom on Valentine's Day."

"Fantastic idea!" Another parent spoke out. "It will be a successful fundraiser!"

I felt inspired to introduce new ideas to the committee. These were some of the same fundraisers my church and school did when I was growing up.

It was Melissa's bright idea that I become a member of the PTA at our daughters' school. It didn't take long before they voted me president of the fundraising committee. When I first joined, I would watch the parents confidently come and go and talk amongst one another. I was barely able to hold a regular conversation without feeling awkward. It made me realize how secluded I had become all these years, but I enjoyed doing something new for myself and was finally using my skills outside of the house.

"You were amazing!" Melissa said as we sat at the local cafe drinking tea.

"I sounded like I was stumbling over my words," I said sheepishly.

"No, ma'am! You owned that room. You brought new ways to bring money to the committee, and the kids will have fun participating."

"Thank you," I smiled, receiving the compliments.

"Hey! I need a favor," I told her.

"Sure. What's up?" Melissa asked.

"I need to buy new, up-to-date clothes, starting with a fall wardrobe. I haven't purchased new clothes in years," I admitted. "It was ok when I wasn't leaving the house much, but looking around at these women, I feel like a hot mess in these rags," I laughed embarrassingly.

"You do not look like a hot mess!" Melissa laughed. "But you know I don't need any reason to go shopping!"

"We should go to that new mall on the other side of town this weekend," I suggested. "Have you been?"

"No, but I've heard about it from a few neighbors," she said. "I think it will be fun. We can bring the girls, too."

****

Mia and Tai laughed in the back seat as Melissa did, and I sat up front talking. Mia was happy to be going out more and enjoying life, and so was I. The ride to the mall was just over an hour. The parking lot was full of cars and busy with people hurrying about.

Mia and Tai walked ahead quickly to get out of the cold, leaving us behind.

"Don't go too far, girls," Melissa called out.

"This is a pretty fancy mall," I said, looking at the grand entrance.

"Yes, that's what my neighbor said," Melissa responded. "Fancy and high end."

The aroma of fresh coffee hit our noses as we stepped up to the automatic glass doors that opened wide for us. We were quickly distracted by the smells, the lights, the mannequins in the windows dressed in fancy clothes. We almost lost track of the girls.

"Don't worry. They can't get too far," Melissa said, heading straight for the coffee shop.

My nerves were on edge as I scanned the crowd for them.

****

"Which way is the ice cream parlor in here?" Tai shouted, looking around. Mia laughed at her outburst.

"Girl, how am I supposed to know?"

"Hey! Are you with an adult?" a male's voice called out.

"Hey!" he called out again, catching Tai's attention. They both turned to find a young man dressed in an all-black security uniform.

"Yes, sir?" Tia answered.

"Are you with an adult?" the security guard said harshly. Mia looked at him and could feel his anger growing. Confused by his aggression, she looked to see if their moms were near.

"Our parents are on their way in," Mia said softly. "Would you like us to wait here until they arrive?"

"Yeah, we don't need any problems from your kind in here."

The man looked at them with an anger that Mia could not place, and she felt the hair on the back of her neck stand up. Tai's facial expression had gone from jovial to afraid, which made Mia even more upset.

"They should be coming in soon, sir. We will sit right here with you. Is that ok?" Mia asked him.

"Sure," he responded, confused by Mia's calm reaction.

Tai sat on the bench, staring into the crowd with her eyes filled with tears.

"I heard this is quite a fancy mall. Do you like working here?" Mia asked him, looking him in the eyes as she spoke.

"Yeah, it's alright," he said, shifting back and forth.

"I can imagine it being hard to watch over all these people. That's a lot of responsibility." The man could not break the eye contact Mia had on him.

"Yeah, it can be a little stressful," he responded in a softer tone.

"Well, I think you are doing an awesome job. Especially how you treat each person who enters the mall with so much respect."

The guard nodded his head and smiled.

"Well, thank you!" he said. "I treat each person with respect, no matter who they are."

Mia looked over at Tai, who now had a slight smile on her face.

"I see our parents," Mia pointed. Tai ran to her mother, and the guard walked over, too.

"I was afraid these young ladies may have gotten lost in the mall, so I waited with them to make sure they could find you."

He walked away, somewhat disoriented. I looked over at Mia and gave her a wink and a smile.

"What was that all about?" Melissa asked Tai, sensing something off about the situation.

Mia shrugged her shoulders as she stood beside Tai and held her hand.

Chapter 16 - Powerless Powers

I was settling into the flow of middle school, getting good grades, and spending time with Tai. Mommy was busy with the PTA and feeling good in her new clothes. After school, I would play with my powers as I discovered more about my abilities.

The winter came fast and hard. The bitter cold made it impossible to be outside much this year. It was more brutal than the state had encountered in decades. Temperatures had fallen to -22 degrees Fahrenheit and remained there for over a week, forcing schools to close and canceling all extra-curricular activities. That didn't happen often in Moscow, Idaho.

Mommy and I were used to keeping each other busy from the years I was homeschooled. We pulled out the board games, including Scrabble. I was always amazed at how many words she could come up with. We also had fun pampering each other with facials and pedicures. Friday evening, we nailed blankets to the windows to keep out the draft and snuggled up to watch movies all night with wood burning in the fireplace.

The phone rang. We both knew who it was.

"Hey, my love," Mommy flirted, as she always did when she knew it was her husband.

"I am on my way home. The weather is bad, so it may take me a little longer," I heard Daddy say.

"Do you think you should wait out the storm?" Mommy asked.

"Nah, I should be good," he assured me.

"Ok. Be safe. I love you."

"Love you back," he said to her before ending the call.

I know she was looking forward to seeing him. He had been gone for two weeks this time. After we moved to Idaho, Daddy's job put a physical distance between them that they hadn't had since he was in college. And 20 years later, there is still magic. They talk every day before bed, just like high school sweethearts. I could tell that it bothered her when he was away too long. She deeply missed seeing her best friend every day.

****

The wind howled loudly, so loudly that it woke me. The wind sounded like someone was crying. I sat up and touched my dampened face. My heart was racing. I looked around the dark room lit only by the smoldering pits in the fireplace.

"Mommy," I tapped her vigorously. "Mommy," I called out again.

She finally woke up.

"Yes, what's wrong?" she mumbled, adjusting her eyes to the darkness.

"Somethings wrong with Daddy." I couldn't keep my voice from trembling. She sat upright.

"Something's wrong. Call Daddy, please."

Now fully awake, she looked at the clock on her phone—3:35 a.m.

"He should have been home by now," she said as she pushed send on the last number called with shaking hands.

"You've reached John..." the voicemail started. She disconnected the call and tried again several times, but it went straight to voicemail each time.

The knock at the door startled us both. With her phone still in hand, she got up.

"That must be him," Mommy said with a sigh of relief.

"Why would he be knocking?" I asked.

"He must have lost his keys or something," she said while wrapping a blanket around her and walking towards the door with me on her heels.

My heart broke for her as I could hear her thoughts. I knew she didn't think it was him knocking.

The officer's badge shined bright when the door opened.

"Mrs. Price?"

"Yes."

We stood with the door open and stared at the white man in a hooded dark green uniform coat.

"Your husband's car went off the side of the road..."

I watched my mother as she listened to the officer tell her that the love of her life was dead. She listened as he finished his speech in a melancholy voice.

"I am very sorry for your loss," he said as she closed the door. She staggered back to the living room and sat on his favorite spot on the couch.

"He's gone, Mia?" she asked me. "Did he just say my husband is never coming back? What am I going to do?"

She then let out a scream that filled the entire house, a sound I will never forget. The pain I felt for and from her was immense. The tears wouldn't come for me despite the heaviness in my heart. I had already known that my father was gone, and I needed to be strong for her. I held her in silence for the next few hours in the cold house, where the wood in the fireplace had all burned out.

****

The funeral was arranged quickly and quietly since we didn't know many people in Idaho, and only small amounts of family were able to travel for the services. After everyone left, Mommy sat in the front pew of the church, and I stood at the side of the closed casket.

"I'm so sorry I couldn't help you, Daddy. I could reach everyone else but couldn't help you," I cried quietly. "Why do I have this power if I can't help the ones I love?"

Mommy came to my side, rubbing my shoulders.

"Please don't blame yourself, sweetie. God had his plans."

"Well, I don't like his plans!" I turned around and cried into my mother's chest.

"Some things we can't control. When you showed up on our porch, it was like a miracle, and we knew that we had to give you the world, and you gave us a chance at a new life. That was not planned either. We will be ok! I promise you."

I looked at my mother and felt strength in her that had not been there before.

"We will be ok!" she repeated.

Later that night, I couldn't sleep. I tossed and turned in my bed. Even though Daddy wasn't home often, his presence was always there. But tonight, I couldn't feel it. I didn't feel his spirit. The house felt hollow and empty, almost eerie. I got up to look out of the frost-covered window. Staring out into our seemingly endless land, where the sky touched the earth, had become one of my favorite pastimes. The view of the green prairie in the spring and the snow in the winter was the best part about living here. I looked past the icicles which hung from the gutters. I saw the moon hiding in the darkness behind a few clouds tonight. I opened my window to get a better view, and the chilling cold hit my face. Just then, I thought I saw a twinkling star. It began to shine brighter and brighter. I was amazed and couldn't turn away. I felt a sense of peace come over me.

I whispered, "Help me. Help me, please. What am I supposed to do now? What am I supposed to do with these powers if I couldn't use them to save my daddy? What are we gonna do without him?"

I took a deep breath of the winter air and closed my eyes. "Please guide me."

I don't know if I was talking to the moon, the twinkling star, or the cold, dark emptiness. I wanted to hear someone talk back and tell me everything would be okay. I wanted to hear my daddy's voice, too. I listened and listened, but I heard nothing except the chilly wind blowing into my room.

"Forget this. It's too cold," I said, closing the window and climbing back under my mountain of blankets.

As I warmed up and closed my eyes, I heard an unfamiliar voice say, "This is happening now for something you're supposed to do later!"

My eyes opened wide. The howling wind picked up, and the windows began to shake. I swiftly went to look out the window and saw words written in the frost.

"I AM Mia."

"Thank you, Daddy," I whispered, feeling joy.

Chapter 17 –The Long Ride Home

Because John was the primary provider, things got financially rough rather quickly. The life insurance policy covered the burial expenses and kept us above water with bills for only a few months. I hadn't worked since my short time at the post office many years ago, so getting a job that maintained our lifestyle was demanding.

John's family and some of our friends, including Melissa, were generous enough to give us the money to move back to Ohio to live with my mother. Mia and I skillfully stuffed as many items that fit into four suitcases. Enough to hold us over until the moving truck brought the rest of our belongings later that month. Heartbroken and afraid, we said goodbye to our tiny house and left Idaho.

****

The bus trip across the country allowed me to update Mia about the grandmother she had never met and whom I had not spoken to in years and had never spoken to her.

"Mama is a strong-willed woman, stronger than anyone I have ever met. I don't think I have ever seen her cry," I smiled, reflecting on a few of my good memories with her.

"But her strength came at a cost to me that caused a lot of barriers for me as her only child. She didn't want to coddle me too much because she didn't want me to be soft."

My smile disappeared as the good memories faded and the painful ones resurfaced.

"Black women have no room for weakness," she would tell me.

"School was my first and last priority. I wasn't allowed to have many friends because she didn't trust people. I earned all A's and received every award that the school offered. I was the perfect student in the eyes of my teachers. But every day, I went home sad and alone. Mama had even made up her mind about where I was going to college after I graduated from high school. Nothing less than Princeton for my daughter," she would tell the other parents.

"But I knew by the 9th grade that I would be gone. For years, I saved money from birthday gifts and chores, planning to move out as soon as I graduated. The day after graduation, I packed one bag and left in the middle of the night, leaving over $50,000 in scholarships on the table. I was 18 years old and didn't need her permission anymore, but I was still too afraid to face her.

"John convinced me to call her after we married for several years. With his support, I could tell her why I left home. Our relationship was beyond repair by then, but we settled on giving each other birthday cards and calling for the holidays. Eventually, that stopped, too. I haven't spoken to her in over 15 years."

Mia was stunned. "So what you're saying is I have a grandmother you never told me about?"

I nodded my head shamefully. "Yes, and I'm embarrassed and ashamed to admit that."

"Why didn't you tell me?"

"Because you would have wanted to meet her, and I couldn't bring myself to deal with her criticism of how she thought my life should be. Eighteen years was hard enough, and I still don't feel I have recovered."

"What about your dad? Who is he?" Mia asked, more curious about this unknown family.

"I never knew who he was, and Mama refused to talk about him."

"Well, dang, this is going to be interesting," Mia said jokingly. I couldn't help but chuckle at her response.

"Yeah, I guess it will be." We both laughed, but inwardly, I was apprehensive about what would come.

The remainder of the bus ride was long and uneventful. Mia rode with her headphones on to drown out the voices of the people on the bus. She had come to find music to be a place of comfort to calm her mind when in crowded places.

As we passed miles and miles of plain flatlands and wheat fields, I knew we were closer to home. Mia was tired, so she allowed herself to drift off to sleep.

"Mia, we are coming up on a stop soon," I said, nudging her.

After a few minutes, I nudged her again.

"Mia, wake up," I said, gently lifting an earphone off her right ear so she could hear me.

She didn't respond.

"Are you ok, Mia?" I brushed my hand across her forehead and took her earphones off. "Please don't do this to me now!" I said, trying not to make a scene.

Chapter 18 - Jamil X

The bus trip to Ohio had to be the most traumatic ride of my life. We spent two days on the road with random strangers, multiple energies, thoughts, and smells. But it gave Mommy and me plenty of time to talk, with even more time to spare. Luckily, I had my new headphones to tune out most of the noise.

Neither the long ride nor the headphones could distract me from thinking about all I had just lost and all the unknown factors ahead of me. Everything I had known for the last 8 years was gone or packed in boxes and shipped back to Ohio to a home I had never been to. Now I'm headed to meet a grandmother I never knew existed; after hearing Mommy talk about her, I'm not sure I wanted to. But I kept an open mind and heart.

Once I could fall asleep again, something I did little of during the ride, Mommy woke me by calling my name.

"Mia, we are coming up on a stop soon."

"Mia, wake up," she called out to me again. "Are you ok?"

I could hear her, but I was no longer on the bus when I opened my eyes. The room was dark and damp, and I could not see in front of me. The smell was dusty and thick, and it took over my senses. I tried to adjust my eyes, but it was of no consequence. I could hear low, shallow breathing in the distance. I then realized I wasn't sleeping but had been teleported to another place.

"Mommy must be worried sick," I thought to myself.

"Who's there?" I called out, frightened by the sudden transport. The room was quiet. "Who's there?" I asked again. "I can feel you there; please say something. Where am I?"

I could faintly hear Mommy calling my name, but I did not want to break the teleport.

"Please tell me who you are. I want to help you."

"My name is Jamil," the faint voice whispered. I've been here a long time," he said. "Can you please get me out of here?"

I could hear Mommy's voice becoming more panicked, and I wanted to tell her I was ok.

"I'll come back and find you, Jamil. I promise," I told him. I could feel his heart beginning to race.

"Please don't leave me," he whispered back with urgency.

"I will be back. I promise! I must tell my mom I'm ok before she panics!"

My eyes opened slowly, adjusting to the light.

"I'm ok, Mommy," I said, holding her hand. "I was with someone who needed my help."

Her heart calmed slowly. "No matter how often you tell me about these episodes, I don't quite understand, and it still frightens me," she said, trying to smile.

"I need to get back to him. I will be ok," I reassured her.

"Okay, but don't be gone long."

I closed my eyes again and was back in the dark and creepy room, now lit by a small light coming in through a crack in the ceiling.

"Jamil," I called out to him. "Are you here?"

"Yes. I've been here a long time," he answered back. "Please get me out of here."

I could see his silhouette in the faint light as he sat on the floor in the corner of the room with his knees pulled to his chest. He appeared smaller than I thought he would, and I could feel his fear.

"Don't be afraid. I'm not here to hurt you," I said, moving closer to him.

"I've been here a long time, and they won't let me leave," he repeated.

"How long have you been here?" I asked.

"Exactly 3832 days, 231,720 minutes, 13,903,200 seconds," he counted.

"Ok, I understand," I said. "You've been here too long!"

Jamil scooted further into the light. I could see his amber-colored eyes, a color I had never seen on a human person. His eyes were filled with sadness.

"I know you can get me out of here. I know who you are," Jamil said.

"How do you know who I am?" I replied, shocked by his statement.

"We all know who you are," he said.

"We? Who are we?" I asked.

"I don't have time to talk about that right now. Please get me out of here. I know you can."

I looked around at what I could make out in the darkened room. The task proved harder than I had imagined. All the doors and exits to the room were padded with multiple thick layers.

"Up there." Jamil pointed toward the ceiling at the small light that came through a thinly opened crack. I looked up to where he pointed to try to see.

"Up there," he pointed again, "is an opening where they send the camera and drone to send me food and different things."

"Through the ceiling?" I asked, looking confused.

"But why?" I asked him. "Why are you in such a dark, closed place?" Something did not feel right.

"We don't have time to talk about that right now," he pleaded. "Please get me out of here. I know you can."

I tried to focus my eyes on the corner where he sat to see if I could make eye contact with him and see into his mind for some answers.

"Don't try to read my mind! You didn't ask me if you could do that!" he yelled.

"I'm sorry," I said, startled by his reaction.

"It's ok. I'm sorry for getting angry, but you didn't ask for permission. I wouldn't say I like that. They never ask for permission either," Jamil said, defeated.

"I know you can read minds because I can read yours. Only a few of us can do that."

"Us?" I questioned again. "There are more of us?"

"You seem to be surprised," Jamil said, laughing intensely. "Yes, there are a lot of us."

I went back to focusing on how I could get him out, but I could feel myself slipping away. No matter how hard I fought it, my mind could no longer keep me there.

"I don't know what's happening, Jamil. I am losing my power here."

"Don't go," he cried out to me. His voice was shaking.

"I'm trying not to, but something is pushing me out!"

"Please don't go!" Jamil cried out again.

"I don't know what's happening. This has never happened before," I said as I faded away.

"Please!"

I heard him cry out, but I was powerless in the space he was being held in.

As I returned, my eyes and body shot straight up in the seat. I gasped for air so forcefully that it startled my mother and the people sitting near me.

"Mia, what's wrong?" Mommy asked.

I was breathing hard, and my eyes felt like a wild cat.

"I couldn't help him," I said, breathing heavily. "The force around him was powerful! He was so scared, and I couldn't help him! I'm not sure what to do. I can't help him! Just like Daddy, I couldn't help him!" Mommy held me as I sobbed.

The bus came to a much-needed rest stop. As each person walked off, I could feel them staring at me and hear some of their thoughts. "Poor child," one man said while shaking his head with pity.

I lay in my mother's arms and waited for the bus to fill back up with all the voices. I rode the remainder of the ride in silence, thinking. How did he know my name? If there are more like us, where can I find them?

****

The long ride was finally over as the bus pulled into the bus depot in Cleveland. The chill on the windows was as uninviting as it was in Moscow. I helped Mommy with the four large suitcases we were allowed to bring on the bus. We stood silently outside against the wall, feeling anxious while we waited. I thought of Jamil locked away, and Mommy worried about seeing her Mama for the first time in over 15 years.

Soon, a large old red van pulled up to the curb. A woman with bouncy, curly brown hair was at the wheel. She was so short she could barely see over the steering wheel. She rolled the window down and yelled out.

"Y'all, come on, it's cold out here!"

Mommy and I looked at one another simultaneously, shrugged shoulders, grabbed our suitcases, and loaded the van.

After about 15 minutes of riding in silence, the woman asked, "Are you hungry?"

I was too afraid to answer.

"Speak up!" she fired again. "A closed mouth don't get fed!"

"Yes, ma'am," Mommy responded. I could hear the fear in her voice and touched her hand softly.

"There's peas and rice on the stove when we get home. You're welcome to them," she said, keeping her eyes on the road.

I walked into the house with utter excitement at its size.

"Wow! This house is huge!" I dropped my bag and began to wander around.

"It's like a big ole mansion from the old days!" I said, turning in circles. "We ain't never had this much space!"

"Your room is where it was the last time you were here," the woman said, nodding toward the stairs. "The little girl can put her things in the guest room."

"Her name is Mia," Mommy said quietly.

"What do you say, girl? Speak up!"

Mommy turned around, "My daughter, your granddaughter's name is Mia."

"Oh, okay then. *Mia* can stay in the guest room," the woman shot back.

I could feel the tension rising. "Thank you!" I said to her, "Your home is beeaauutifulll!!!

I sang the words while grabbing my suitcase and bag and heading for the stairs.

Oh, and what should I call you?" I asked her before heading up.

"Call me? She asked.

"Yes, what name should I call you?

"Well, I hadn't thought about that," she paused. "I guess you can call me Lily."

"Great!" I said. Granny Lily!" I squealed and walked towards the stairs leading to the guest room. "Granny Lily, Granny Lily, Granny Lily," I sang repeatedly, dragging my suitcase up each step.

Mommy and Granny Lily both couldn't help but laugh.

The first night in my new house was hard. The room was set up like a guest room that never saw guests— there was no real love to it. It was furnished with a bed, dresser, desk, chair, and a nightstand with a small lamp. There was a picture in a frame on the nightstand, but it was a fake picture—one that comes in the frame when you buy it from the store.

The house was quiet and had a light chill. I was used to the cold of Idaho, but this chill felt internal. The ride was long and draining, but I couldn't sleep. I stared a hole through the ceiling while lying in my new bed before finally drifting off to sleep.

The window rattled and shook me awake, and a chill ran through me. I could feel it moving through my body, but I was not moving.

"You said you would come back for me," a low voice scowled.

The windows rattled louder, but I could not move; my body was frozen. The harder I tried to move, the heavier the force held me in place.

"You said you would come back for me! You promised!"

"Jamil?" I called out.

The windows rattled ferociously, and the wind began to howl. I could see the last remaining leaves swaying on the trees in the streetlight shadows.

"You didn't come back for me. Why did you lie to me?" Jamil's voice came low and angry. I was almost too afraid to speak.

"I tried," I finally said.

"You shouldn't make promises you can't keep! You're just like them!" he cried out.

Just as suddenly as he came, he was gone, and I was freed from the cold force. The wind calmed, and the room was steady. I pulled the blankets over my head, knowing that not even the biggest blanket could have helped me.

"I'm not like them," I said aloud. "I don't even know who *they* are!"

"Who are you talking to?" Granny Lily called from the doorway. I was startled by her sudden appearance and unsure how long she had been standing there.

"You must have little imaginary friends like your Mama used to have," she said, shaking her head. Without waiting for an answer, she closed the door. I was relieved that I didn't have to explain.

I tried to settle back to sleep, but Jamil needed me, and I needed to figure out how to help him.

Chapter 19 - New Beginnings

Even though I hadn't been to Cleveland since kindergarten, I remembered everything. I recognized the sounds and smells. I remembered the buildings and houses as we ran errands around the city. Some of the memories brought comfort, and some brought sadness.

We arrived at my new middle school just after lunch, and the office was busy with students and staff. Mommy went from one room to the next doing the registration paperwork. Everyone bustled past me as I sat on the wooden bench watching. Some students stared, while others completely ignored me. I attempted to turn off my senses that read each person in the area, but it was in vain. I spent the remaining time shifting on the hard bench, staring at the floor, trying to ignore all the information I received from my new classmates.

As I continued to wait, I heard a clock ticking abnormally loud—so loud that it forced me to look up and find where it was coming from. The ticking became louder, drawing my attention to the far-right corner of the office, where three doors were located. I strained my eyes to make out the names on the black plates of each door.

"Mrs. Thompson, Counselor."

"Mr. Griffin, Asst. Principal."

The clock was centered directly over the last door. The nameplate reads, "Dr. Sekou, Counselor."

Just then, Mommy tapped me on my shoulder. "Mia, we're done."

"Thank goodness!" I thought, quickly standing ready to go.

We left the office, and I glanced back at Dr. Sekou's closed door.

"You will start school next Monday," Mommy said as we walked to the car. She fiddled through the pile of forms and documents from the office.

"Yay, me," I responded sarcastically as I followed closely behind.

Mommy turned and looked at me.

"I know this has been a hard transition for you," she said.

"I'm just kidding, Mommy." I lied and gave as big of a smile as I could. I didn't want to upset her with my true feelings.

"Did you know that Dr. Sekou works at this school?"

Mommy stopped in her tracks. "Where? Did you see him? Did you speak to him?"

I chuckled at the way she rattled off the questions. "No, I saw his name on the door in the office."

"That might not be the same person," she said as she started walking again.

"It's him, I can feel it."

She stopped walking again and turned to me. "Please be careful who you talk to, Mia," she pleaded. "You don't know these people, and I don't want anything to happen to you."

"I know, I will be careful," I assured her.

In my heart, I knew that I would have to speak with him. He was the scientist who had researched my extraordinary abilities, but I'm not sure how he became a school counselor.

****

Each night, the windows rattled, and Granny Lily was amused every time she caught me talking to myself. The weekend came and went fast, seemingly 'in the blink of an eye,' as Mommy always said. Monday morning was there, and my new school was waiting.

"Wake up, little girl," Granny Lily opened the door without knocking. To her surprise, I was already dressed.

"Good morning, Granny Lily," I called back, spinning around in circles in the white swivel chair in my room.

She looked surprised. "Oh, you're already up?"

"Yes, ma'am, yes, ma'am!" I swirled around again. She didn't know that the sound of the rattling windows kept me up all night. She shook her head and told me to come downstairs for breakfast.

Here I go again with a new bus, new kids, and new beginnings. This time, I was painfully uneasy about all of the newness. My love of adventure had faded.

The school bus was different from the one in Idaho. When it arrived, it was full, with almost no seats available. Once again, I am trying to figure out where to sit and how to fit in. The bus driver, a heavy-set woman with a thin mustache, made the decision easy for me.

"You have an assigned seat and will sit there daily. No swapping seats, no loud talking, face forward, and no fighting, or you will be put off this bus, and your parents will have to figure out how to get you to school. Do you understand?" she asked.

I must have looked perplexed because the driver said, "Girl, do you hear me?"

I snapped out of it and replied, "Yes, ma'am," and walked to the seat she pointed to.

"Thank you," she said in a gruff voice.

I sat down and held on to the back of the seat in front of me as the bus pulled off. A boy with an NFL jersey with the number 23 on it was already sitting by the window.

"Hi," he greeted. "I'm Al. Are you new?"

"Yes! Unfortunately, I am!" I exclaimed.

He laughed kindly, which made me relax and sit back for the ride.

****

Navigating the crowded hallways and chatter from the numerous students was quite challenging. The noise and activity were more than I had expected or had previously experienced. Not only did I hear it externally via my ears, but I also heard information about many kids inside my head. I decided to find the nearest bathroom instead of going to homeroom. Cutting class on my first day was not a great way to start at a new school. I locked myself in a stall and looked at the scribbles on the walls. The quietness of the bathroom was welcoming, and I sat there for a while.

I felt the warmth of the first tear fall and was startled because I rarely cried and didn't feel it coming. More followed, and I did not try to stop them. A part of me knew I needed to let it out. Each tear felt like a relief. For my Daddy's death, for missing my best friend Tai, for leaving our home in Idaho, for the pain I felt from Mommy missing Daddy and her struggles with Granny Lily.

Strangely, the silent release of tears gave me the energy to get through the rest of the day.

****

I made it through day one but had no idea where to catch my bus after school. I followed the other students to the bus line and looked for familiar faces from the morning ride. I didn't recognize anyone in the sea of students. I didn't even see Al with his NFL jersey on.

"Excuse me, sir," I said as I tapped the shoulder of a man holding a clipboard near the bus line.

"Yes," he turned around. I looked up at his face, then down at his badge.

"Dr. Sekou?"

"How can I help you?" he asked.

"Do you remember me?" I asked." My name is Mia, Mia Price."

"I'm sorry there are so many students here; it's hard to keep track," he said with a warm-hearted smile.

"Did we have a counseling appointment today?" he asked.

"No," I said, puzzled. "Can you tell me what bus goes to East 113th and Kingsman?"

He looked down at his clipboard and answered, "Bus #602."

He pointed me in the direction of the correct bus. I walked away, disappointed that he didn't remember me.

Coming home from school after my first day would be different this time. Mommy wouldn't be home to greet me as she had been on my previous first days. She had gotten two jobs: one at the Post Office and a weekend position as a cashier at the corner store. Our lives had changed so much, and I didn't know what to expect anymore.

Granny Lily was in the living room, watching Judge TV, and the house smelled of spices and baked goods.

"Hi, Granny Lily," I said dryly.

"Hey girl, how was your day?"

"Meh," I responded as I walked upstairs to my new room, closed the door behind me, and flopped down on my bed.

I heard a light tap at the door, and Granny Lily peeked in.

"You want some cookies, little girl?" she asked affectionately.

"Yes," I smiled back. "Yes, I would love some cookies."

****

The end of my first week of school was close, and I was looking forward to it. Mommy and I had planned a Girl's Day since she had been working so much and we hadn't spent much time together.

When the final bell rang, the halls were hectic as I walked to my locker to get my coat and put my books inside.

As I opened the locker, a small piece of paper fell out. I picked it up and saw the front of it read "Mia." I suddenly felt an overwhelming feeling of being watched. I tucked the note into the pocket of my book bag, closed the locker, and walked outside to catch my bus. I chose to wait until I got home to read the note. The bus ride seemed to take forever.

When my stop came, I exited quickly and ran through the front door of Granny Lily's big house.

"Hey, Granny Lily," I waved as I hurried up the stairs.

"Why are you running, little girl?" she asked from her favorite chair.

"No reason. Be right back!" I responded, closing the door behind me and pulling the note from my book bag.

"If **Y**ou **I**nvest **R**ight, **Y**ou **W**ill **N**ever **T**ake **M**oney. **30**% Education, **30**% Real Estate."

"What?" I asked myself. I stared at the note for a few minutes and decided it was mistakenly put in my locker. I crumpled it up and threw it into the trash can. Then I went to join Granny Lily for Pie and Judge TV.

****

Dinner with Mommy and Granny was still silently awkward, so I excused myself from the table early.

"What time are we leaving tomorrow?" I asked Mommy as I got up to take my plate to the kitchen.

"Where are y'all going?" Granny Lily blurted out. I think she shocked herself by asking.

"We're having Girl's Day. Do you wanna come?" I offered.

Mommy cleared her throat and adjusted herself in the seat.

"Nah, that's okay," Granny Lily responded. "Y'all go ahead without me."

I could tell she wanted to go. She was always in the house alone. I looked over at Mommy, who was now staring at her fork.

Mommy hesitated and said, "You should come with us. It will be fun."

"Sure, ok, I'll come," said Granny Lily with a slight grin.

"See, Granny, now we can all go! Girl's Day, Girl's Day!"

I knew Mommy wasn't happy Granny Lily was coming with us, but we had to start somewhere. I skipped playfully back to my room, excited at the thought of us being able to hang out together. I was looking forward to them getting along better.

****

As we drove to our first stop on Girl's Day, the vibe between Mommy and Granny Lily was unpleasant as usual. Mommy looked stressed, and Granny Lily gripped the steering wheel so tightly that her knuckles were white.

"What would you like to eat, Granny Lily?" I asked, breaking the silence.

"It doesn't matter to me, little girl," Granny responded. "Food is food."

"Her name is Mia," Mommy said in a stern voice.

"What?" Granny questioned, looking over at Mommy.

"Her name is Mia, not girl," Mommy snapped back.

"Who do you think you are talking to?" Granny Lily asked rhetorically, staring at her coldly, no longer looking at the road.

"You! Please call her by her name!" she yelled.

I was taken aback. I had never heard Mommy yell before.

"It's ok, Mommy," I interjected.

"You think you can talk to me like that in my car?" Granny Lily fumed as she braked for a stop light.

I could feel their hearts pounding as the argument escalated with the raw emotions they had bottled up for a long time.

"We can get out of your car!" Mommy screamed, her voice cracking. You can't tell me what to do anymore!"

"Then you don't need to be in my house, right?" Granny Lily fired.

Mommy was crying and heaving. She looked at me and quieted down for a moment. I knew she was choosing her next words very carefully.

"I don't hear your smart mouth now," Granny Lily continued to strike back.

All I wanted to do was melt into the seat and disappear. Maybe this wasn't such a good idea. They were so angry with one another. My hands became hot, and my eyes began to burn. I took a deep breath and slowly exhaled.

"Calm the energy in this space," I whispered in the air. I took another full, deep breath and exhaled. "Calm the energy in this space."

The music on the radio gradually got louder, drowning out the voices of Granny, Lily, and Mommy. We listened to smooth jazz and rode to the restaurant without talking.

We sat and ate lunch somberly. No one talked except to order the food. The nail tech could tell something was wrong when we got to the nail salon. She tried to lighten the mood, but nothing came out of those two women except tension. Girl's Day was an epic fail. We decided to end the Girl's Day and go home earlier than planned. Luckily, it was winter, and the night came sooner than later. I was happy to go straight to bed after such a draining day.

I noticed the door was closed as I approached my room, although I had left it open when I went downstairs earlier. I slowly entered and saw the note I threw in the trash can, now on my pillow. I turned on the light, and the feeling of being watched came over me again. I closed the door behind me and looked around the room before I picked up the note.

"If **Y**ou **I**nvest **R**ight, **Y**ou **W**ill **N**ever **T**ake **M**oney. **30**% Education, **30**% Real Estate."

"Oh wow! This is written in code!"

"**Y**es, **I R**emember **Y**ou. **W**e **N**eed **T**o **M**eet at **3:30** p.m. at the school building."

It was Dr. Sekou.